W. R. Guilfoyle

Annual report on the Melbourne Botanic Gardens

Government House grounds and Domain

W. R. Guilfoyle

Annual report on the Melbourne Botanic Gardens
Government House grounds and Domain

ISBN/EAN: 9783741198113

Manufactured in Europe, USA, Canada, Australia, Japa

Cover: Foto ©Andreas Hilbeck / pixelio.de

Manufactured and distributed by brebook publishing software
(www.brebook.com)

W. R. Guilfoyle

Annual report on the Melbourne Botanic Gardens

Melbourne Botanic and Domain Gardens, Victoria.

ANNUAL REPORT

ON THE

MELBOURNE BOTANIC GARDENS,

GOVERNMENT HOUSE GROUNDS AND DOMAIN.

BY

W. R. GUILFOYLE, F.L.S., C.M.R.B.S., LONDON,
CURATOR.

MELBOURNE:
BY AUTHORITY: JOHN FERRES, GOVERNMENT PRINTER.

M DCCC LXXVII.

ANNUAL REPORT

OF THE CURATOR OF THE

BOTANIC AND DOMAIN GARDENS, MELBOURNE.

TO THE HONORABLE FRANCIS LONGMORE, M.P., MINISTER FOR
LANDS AND AGRICULTURE, ETC., ETC.

Botanic Gardens,

SIR, Melbourne, 25th June, 1877.

I have the honor to submit herewith my Fourth Annual Progress
Report on the Botanical and Domain Gardens, dating from July 1876.

The general work accomplished in the Botanic Gardens during the
financial year has been considerable. Though the weather at times
proved very adverse—one flood in particular doing much damage—
operations steadily continued. The extra laborers allowed last year
(12 in number) enabled me to make great advances in my general
design for remodelling these grounds. It is to this temporary and
extraneous source of labor that I have in a great measure to look for
accomplishing the work of renovation ; the regular staff being mainly
employed in keeping the Gardens in order. Should the same amount
of assistance be granted in the future, the completion of the Botanic
Gardens will be most materially forwarded.

The whole of the men employed in the Gardens now work on a
departmental system, which has taken some time and experience to
perfect. It is most satisfactory in its results. By this means an
increased sense of responsibility is created, and a healthy spirit of
emulation excited. Speaking collectively, the staff deserve commenda-
tion for the manner in which their duties were performed during the
year.

In the draft estimates forwarded by me for the ensuing financial year
there is a total decrease of £620, as compared with last year, on the
amount for the Garden and Domain.

It is highly desirable that on entering a Botanic Garden visitors
should at once recognise the purpose to which the grounds are devoted, by seeing groups arranged according to their botanical order.

Thoroughly appreciating this fact, I have continuously held in view the production throughout the Gardens of a classified system, which, instead of being dwarfed by localisation to one particular spot, should be broad, intelligible, and widely spread. In some public gardens the climate would prevent this being done to any material extent ; but such an objection cannot be urged in this colony. No necessity exists for allowing botanical correctness and landscape effect to clash in the development of the Melbourne Botanic Gardens. To combine the two, as I have pointed out in previous reports, has been my design from the beginning ; and that design has been carried out as the work of renovation went on. As stated in my last report, the first group— Amaryllideæ—was completed, near the Band stand, last year. This year, a large number of orders have been grouped in suitable positions, as follow :—

On the new Lawn (8 acres in extent, and made this year) the following have been placed :—Laurineæ, Pittosporeæ, Saxifrageæ, Solaneæ, Proteaceæ, Polygaleæ, Anonaceæ, Magnoliaeeæ, Ranunculaceæ, Urticeæ (including Ulmaceæ, Moraeeæ, Cannabinaeeæ, and Platanaeeæ), Ternstrœmiaceæ, Erieaceæ, Epaeridcæ, Rosaeeæ, Cupuliferæ, Thymeleæ, and Berberidaeeæ. This lawn (which is of larger dimensions than any of the other three in the Botanic Gardens) will have a sward composed of mixed grasses, principally Stenotaphrum glabrum (buffalo grass) ; Cynodon dactylon (couch grass), and English lawn grasses. A judicious mixture of these produces a more elastic, permanently vivid, and beautiful turf than any single species of grass.

On the lawn near the Reservoir, close to Anderson street, the orders Myoporineæ, Acanthaeeæ, Verbenaceæ, Serophularineæ, and Bignoniaeeæ have been grouped. It was necessary for taking the new Conservatory levels to lower the crest of the hill in this spot ; and a triangular piece of lawn was then formed, on which the above orders were grouped. Close to the reservoir is arranged the order of the Jasmineæ, which includes the Fraxinus, &c. The fence enclosing the reservoir has proved useful as a trellis for training the climbing species —such as the Jasmines.

A list of the species belonging to each order as grouped, will be found in Appendix A attached to this report.

The plants representing these and other orders were mostly taken from thickets and other places where they were hidden from view, or scattered promiscuously over the grounds. It is necessary to add that the different species have not been placed in formal beds, but in irregular groups, cut out of the sward; and so arranged that the taller growing specimens are placed in the centre, the shrubs or herbaceous kinds in front.

The curves are so formed that the visitor can read the name of each plant without walking on the beds; and besides the botanical term and authority for it, the vernacular name, habitat, &c., is given upon the label. It is also my intention to place in each particular group a label detailing the general medicinal properties of the order, whether stimulant, febrifugal, demulcent, &c., &c., &c. By thus grouping the different orders, the requisite landscape effect is preserved, while the botanical student's researches are facilitated. Very shortly other important orders will be located in suitable spots, including the Myrtaceæ, Leguminosæ, Liliaceæ, Salacineæ, Betulineæ, Sapindaceæ, Malvaceæ, Tiliaceæ, Sterculiaceæ, Rubiaceæ and Araliaceæ. So far as the work has proceeded, the improved appearance of the Gardens has been fully recognised and acknowledged. The classification and exhaustive catalogue (the latter being nearly completed) will render easy the task of scientific enquirers, whose visits are actuated by other motives than mere admiration for beautiful scenes and landscape pictures.

While on this subject, I may point out that the mere fact of some groups being at present incomplete as collections of the various species, is not to be taken as an indication that the Gardens are altogether deficient in genera which are unrepresented in the groups. It will be readily understood that until the rough work of formation is thoroughly over, a landscape gardener must be very careful in dealing with the sensitive material with which he has to produce his effects. It will also be apparent that while some varieties of plants are sufficiently hardy to be at once placed in the midst of the alterations going on around them, others necessary to complete the group require greater care in the manner and season of transplanting. Having explained the progress made thus far, in making the Botanic Garden really worthy of the name, it only remains to say that when the general design is completed, thousands of very valuable botanic specimens will be planted out in their appropriate localities. I have every confidence that the result will be a garden in which facility of research, and scientific classification, will combine with sterling beauties of landscape scenery.

It is scarcely necessary for me to contradict a statement which has been made, that valuable botanic specimen trees have been destroyed in the course of the improvements effected in these grounds. Every care has been taken of plants which it became necessary to remove; and the

precautions in handling were attended with the greatest possible success.
The collection of valuable specimens is an extremely rich one. It is
being augmented daily ; and when the catalogue (of which the press
copy is now in an advanced state) is issued, it will be found how
unfounded these malicious assertions really are. Plants removed have
always been carefully attended to, and even the smaller shrubs have
been housed, until they could be permanently placed in their appropriate situations. If the necessary funds are granted, it is my intention
immediately to commence a lawn, stretching from the gravel walk at
the lower part of the palm house lawn, to the margin of the lake.
This lawn I purpose planting with the very beautiful orders of
Leguminosæ, and Myrtaceæ—the latter embracing 30 or 40 varieties
of Eucalyptus, Eugenias, &c., &c.—some of them magnificent trees of
towering stature, others dwarfed but pretty bushes, and all alike
charming not only for their foliage but their flowers. Let me briefly
describe one or two species of this order as an indication of the effects
to be produced with such materials at command. First the Syzygium
Moorei (of which I have seen whole forests, in Northern New South
Wales and Queensland) attaining a height of 70 or 80 feet, and
affording when in full bloom, one of the most gorgeous spectacles
imaginable ; its every branch and even a part of the stem, clothed with
one mass of royal purple blossoms, having the appearance of rich pile
velvet. Again, what can be more splendid than the brilliant scarlet
flowers of some of the Callistemons, their numerous and lengthy
filaments giving them the appearance of gorgeous bottle brushes ! The
yellow, lilac, white or pink erect flossy blooms of the Melaleucas,
peeping above their graceful foliage, are objects of great beauty ; and
there are many other genera equally handsome. Even the scarlet and
yellow varieties of the *Eugenia Malaccensis*, which I met with in Fiji
during the cruise of H.M.S. *Challenger*, and which have lately been
added to our collection, might by a little care, be acclimatised, and lend
a charm to the group. The previous existence in this spot of some
large growing species of the order named, and the suitability of the
situation to their successful growth, induced the selection of this locality
in my original design, for the effect to be created. When this work is
accomplished, the lake, now hidden to the view from the upper lawn,
will be seen through glimpses afforded between the groups, and thus
add variety to the scenery. The dwarf shrubs in the classified groups,
backed by the varied foliage and graduated forms of the taller and more
stately species, should form component parts of a Public Garden, which,

from its extent of acreage and great natural capabilities, admits of diversified treatment.

I have spoken of contrasted foliage. The imposing effect of this, even without the adjunct of a single flower, may be seen in an excellent picture (by Sonntag) in the Melbourne National Gallery, entitled "A Scene on the Hudson" showing the remarkable results produced by such combinations. Lower down on this new Lawn, near the margin of the lake, will be placed Salacineæ, Betulineæ, and Sapindaceæ ; such a position being particularly suited to them, as they are lovers of moisture.

The Fern Gully now contains an extensive collection of beautiful plants. Where half a dozen species only were formerly represented, a space about 140 yards in length, with slopes of 50 yards at the widest part, is filled with graceful representatives of the fern kingdom, and species of trees and shrubs loving cool shade and moisture. The arboreal ferns include some magnificent specimens 'of Alsophila Australis, Alsophila excelsa, Dicksonia antarctica, Dicksonia squarrosa, Dicksonia Youngiana, Cyathea medullaris, Cyathea dealbata (silver tree fern), Cyathea Cunninghami and Hemitelia Smithii &c. The dwarf ferns comprise many species of Pteris, Aspidium, Asplenium, Lomaria, Davallia, Acrostichum, Todea, Polypodium, Adiantum, and many others. Plentifully distributed amongst these ferns which are in patches along the water course, and aiding to give a tropical appearance to this sequestered spot, are Cannas, Musa, Alpinias, Callas, Taro, Arundo, Hydrangeas, Gynerium (Pampas grass) Dianellas, Phormium tenax (New Zealand flax) and scores of other plants of a similar character. Amongst the tall trees, (transplanted to afford the requisite shade) are many specimens of Gleditschias, Grevilleas, Pittosporum, Ulmus, Platanus, Ailanthus, Ficus, Tristania, Tamarix, Dammara, Melaleuca, Quercus, and others too numerous to mention. Besides these, are two fine specimens of *Strelitzia Augusta*, one of which had been grown for years in the Palm house ; the other was obtained a few days ago from Mr. Smith, of Adelaide. Upwards of 60 healthy plants of Panax elegans, raised from seed forwarded through the kindness of Walter Hill, Esq., Director of the Brisbane Botanic Gardens, have been placed in the Gully. A number of epiphytal ferns—the Stag-horn and Elk-horn Platyceriums, and the bird's nest Asplenium, received from the same gentleman, have been fixed on the shade trees ; forming capitals to the colonnade of stems. Clinging to these trees are graceful climbers, profusely planted for the purpose of affording a canopy of shade to this tropical dell. Here, also, are to be found several hardy orchids—including Dendrobiums from Northern New South Wales and Queensland. Principal among the climbing plants are Passiflora, Tropæolum, Clematis, Lonchocarpus, Banksian Roses, Tecomas, Wisteria, &c., &c. Some of these graceful plants already hang in festoons from the branches of the shade trees. Judging from their rapid growth, the time is not far distant when they will throw overhead a leafy screen, studded with many hued flowers. Already this spot has proved a great attraction to the visitors, to whom the cool refreshing green of the fern fronds, and the shady aspect, give welcome relief from the fierce glare of the summer sun. Many fine plants of Macrozamia spiralis are distributed through this gully and the adjoining Palmetum, greatly adding to the tropical effect. In the lowest portion or dip of this fernery (where the iron bridge and bird-cages formerly stood), a glimpse is afforded of the rustic bridge spanning the lake. In arranging the Palmetum alluded to I have included the Cycadeæ, as they are closely allied to the Palms ; in fact they are intermediate between the latter and ferns. The classification in question may therefore be considered appropriately placed. The names of the species will be found appended.

The rustic bridge just mentioned was designed principally to break the long line of embankment between the lakes, by bringing together the two promontories, which was done by a one-span arch. Greater variety in the scenery was obtained, by heightening the embankment, and grouping trees and shrubs thereon. At the southern end, a large Pinus halepensis and an Araucaria, together with some Corynocarpus and New Zealand Karaka, form a pretty clump ; while on the opposite side by massing Pittosporums of various shades of green, a few tall Cordylines peeping above them, and drooping to the water's edge a group of Arundo or Danubian reed, the monotony of the scene has thus been relieved.

Several Rockeries have been constructed. Close to the rustic bridge is an extensive one, containing a valuable collection of succulent plants ; such as various species of Opuntia, Cereus, Epiphyllum, Aloes, Yuccas, Agaves, Fourcroya, &c., which were formerly stored in the present fern-house. This house now contains, I have no hesitation in saying, the finest collection of Ferns and Lycopodes in the colony. Care has been taken to secure, by propagation, a supply of the succulent plants represented in the rockeries. The construction of the new bridge was effected by the ordinary labor employed in the Garden, directed by myself ; it is built in a most substantial manner, and the cost (£50) was money well spent, for I will guarantee the bridge lasts for as many years as it has cost pounds. In forming it, two stout stone buttresses were firmly bedded into the clay bottom of the lake, and built up to the requisite height. Four massive beams were then fixed across these buttresses, and the beams planked with stout red gum, bolted to them. On this was laid rongh asphalte, in which orange gravel was embedded. Slanting beams—four in number, placed under the bridge, gave it additional strength. Planks were then nailed to the sides, to support the virgin cork with which the arch is faced. The cork has been arranged in irregular masses, giving the appearance of rock work. The buttresses of moss covered stone, obtained from Yarra bend, blend well with the cork. The rustic railing was made of wood obtained in the grounds, (the material being furnished by superfluous limbs of old gum trees, &c.) strongly attached to the frame work. In constructing this bridge, several matters had to be considered—appearance, economy, and stability. With respect to the first item, the public verdict on that point is satisfactory; so far as stability is concerned, I may mention that the bridge is freely used for the passage of a horse and cart employed in the grounds—a thing absolutely impossible with the former structure. As to economy, the cost was undoubtedly less than a quarter of the sum that would have been asked for in a contract. Added to these facts, I was enabled, by personally directing its construction, to give it the precise appearance I wished, and to get the work done immediately.

The lakes have been kept in order; and the Confervæ mentioned in a previous report practically annihilated. The wild fowl are still plentiful, especially in the open season, when the immunity afforded by this sheet of water seems understood by the birds. The swans, seven in number, are thriving. There are three serious nuisances occasionally experienced in the Garden, in the shape of rabbits, wild cats, and dogs. The rabbits are very numerous and mischievous. They get into the drains, and burrow holes under the foundations of trees. The cats are very destructive to the small birds, particularly the English thrushes. The latter, however, I am glad to say, exist in considerable numbers in the gardens. The dogs hunt both cats and rabbits, and are thus perhaps the greatest nuisance of the trio. I have again to note the kindness of Colonel Anderson in allowing me the use of the pontoon raft to remove a large Pinus halepensis to one of the islands in the lake, where it now forms a conspicuous object in the landscape. Several fine plants of Magnolia grandiflora were also placed on the islands, and additional specimens of the magnificent Eucalyptus ficifolia. The specimens of this tree—the grandest of its tribe—placed last year upon the lake islands, have grown five feet in height; so that in a short time their masses of gorgeous scarlet bloom in the flowering season will add to the attractions of this locality. More than a thousand cart loads of valuable manure were removed from the bed of the large lake, and will be utilised in top dressing the new lawns during the present season. It was fortunate that this was done, as a subsequent severe storm nearly caused the lake to overflow, though it had been materially deepened. The Melaleuca scrub at the head of the large lake is a fine piece of natural scenery, and requires very careful handling. There is most decidedly room for improvement in this spot, as suggested in my last report; by planting palms, Rhododendrons, Magnolias, and other suitable shrubs. Any treatment, however, must be undertaken with great fore-thought and deliberation. Until other portions of the design are com-pleted, this part may well be left in its present state for a time. Progress has to some extent, been made with another classification, the *Coniferæ.* The Pinetum occupies the place where (as described in a previous report) stiff formal rows of trees, seven or eight in number, were planted, a line of Araucaria excelsa being followed by an avenue of Pinus halepensis, succeeded by another row of A. excelsa; then a line of A. Cunninghamii, backed by yet another of A. Bidwilli, the whole presenting a monotonous appearance. All of these superfluous specimens, as they are removed, will be used for decorating other parts of the Garden; and the work of addition will in time render this spot a complete Pinetum.

Five hundred iron labels were written and placed in position during the year. Careful attention was also given to the renewal of old, defective labels. In the same period upwards of 8,000 wooden tallies were prepared and distributed; of which number, over 1,500 were permanently secured by wire fastenings. I regret to say that great annoyance has been caused from time to time by the wilful displacement of labels, evidently the work of some person or persons, not only maliciously disposed, but also remarkably practical in their misappli-cation. Labels have been transposed in such a manner as to give rise to suspicions that none, save those well acquainted with the plants thus misnamed, could effect such ridiculous transpositions; while the manner in which the wire fastenings were adjusted proved the Vandal to possess no prentice hand. Every precaution has been taken to guard against this malignity or senseless practical joking, whichever it may be. Metal labels, with stamped numbers, have been largely employed. Founts of steel type have been procured for stamping names—a system which will ultimately save great time, labor, and expense. The letters will be filled with a preparation of hardened vermilion, producing an agreeable effect.

Two summer houses, or *kiosks*, have been completed, and a third nearly so. The latter stands above the Fern Gully, where the beautiful order of the Lilies will be arranged. All are of a rustic design, constructed of superfluous wood from the wattles lining the Yarra banks. The floors are composed of blocks of wood, laid down in a sort of tessellated pattern, and in a substantial manner. Seats to accommodate 50 persons surround the interior. Two pipes have been laid in the grounds, from which a supply of *Yan Yean* water can be obtained by visitors. Considering the great number of people who visit the Gardens, it is very desirable that drinking fountains should be liberally provided throughout the grounds. There should also be one grand fountain in the centre of the Gardens, forming an attractive feature and supplying a useful purpose. One of the pipes supplies a small fountain near the rustic bridge ; the other is at the entrance gate near the office.

A large portion of the Palm house lawn (which has been increased by several acres) has been planted with groups of Queensland trees which have thriven remarkably well, the ground having previously been carefully drained. These groups have all been labelled with botanical and common names. Labels having a red mark underneath signify that the plant is also indigenous to New South Wales. This geographical distribution has proved very interesting to visitors from the neighboring colonies, enabling them to recognise at one glance many old acquaintances, while the various trees and shrubs, changeful in their hues as they are diversified in size and age, fall agreeably upon the eye as it glances upon them from the unbroken sward.

The floral display during the year appeared to give general satisfaction, and attracted a large share of attention. This matter will of course be properly attended to during the ensuing year. Here I may mention that I have this year asked for two lodges, one to be placed opposite Park street, the other at the principal entrance gate to the Gardens from the St. Kilda road. A third might be advantageously placed at the entrance gate of the Domain, opposite the barracks. The gardeners' houses are at present scattered about the grounds, and are for the most part very unsightly, dilapidated wooden buildings. For the protection of the Gardens it is necessary that these lodges should be built. If neatly designed, they can be made picturesque features in the landscape, as is shown by the red brick lodge which stands near the Yarra bank. The present wooden buildings require constant patching to keep them in repair.

Notwithstanding the occasional heavy rains, and traffic occasioned by the removal of so many large trees from one part of the Garden to another, the new walks have preserved their solidity. The excellent gravel, discovered by sinking, has been extensively used in the formation of walks, which in many instances have replaced others, obliterated in consequence of their uselessness, narrow dimensions, or unsightly shapes. This gravel has proved a very valuable acquisition, retaining the rich orange color which contrasts so agreeably with the green lawns. The principal walks round the four lawns have been finished.

Reference may here be made to another important matter. A number of plants, generally supposed to be unsuited to out door culture in this climate, were successfully placed out in the grounds. Amongst them were " *Quisqualis indica,*" " *Beaumontia grandiflora,*" " *Euphorbia splendens,*" " *Strelitzia augusta,*" " *Strelitzia regina,*" "*Allemanda neriifolia,*" &c. These and many other tropical plants, have proved hardy, growing vigorously outside. The *Alsophila excelsa,* of Norfolk Island, a tree fern which attains the height of 80 feet, has also grown with remarkable rapidity in the open air. As a counterbalance, however, I regret to say that my acticipations respecting the Cinchona (Peruvian Bark) have proved correct—it is an unmitigated failure. I believe that a number of young and strong specimens of this valuable medicinal plant were at one time distributed through this Colony to people in suitable positions for giving every care and attention to them. Yet I have failed to ascertain one instance where the experiment has been attended with success out of doors. On Phillip and French islands, according to reports I have received from gentlemen residing in those localities, some highly tropical plants have maintained life in sheltered positions. But, where a plant can only just manage to exist in certain favorable situations the experiment of acclimatisation looks very like a failure. We have not even this consolation in the case of the Cinchona ; and however valuable a plant may be, it is useless to waste money and time in trying to conquer Nature in such an effort. I repeat my firm belief, that the Cinchona will not grow in Victoria, except cared for in a bush house or shed. But, there are many other valuable plants and trees which are suitable to our climate, and which might be largely cultivated with very important results to the whole country. The Hickory is an instance. By the last mail, I received a large number of Hickory seeds from America. I believe these to be sound ; and from experiments made during the past twelve months, I feel assured this tree will eventually prove a most valuable article of our commerce. Another very valuable plant, the Valonia Oak (*Quercus Ægilops*) has lately caused much public discussion. Judging, however, from the slow growth of the two specimens in the Garden during the last four years (they are scarcely more than two feet high), this tree will take a very long time before it is sufficiently matured to become of commercial value. On the shores of the Mediterranean the acorn cups of this oak produce tannin in large quantities, and of a very valuable nature. Considering, however, the slow growth of the tree, and the improbability on that account of its being extensively cultivated by private enterprise, it might be considered worthy of plantation in the State Forests, or other Government lands ; since if it proved successful, it would eventually form a large source of revenue. Mr. Laurence, who lately introduced seeds of the Valonia Oak, deserves every praise for his experimental effort.

The subject of fodder plants and grasses is one of very great importance to this Colony ; and is therefore deserving of particular notice in a Public Garden, with a view to determining the kinds best adapted for cultivation in various localities. I append a list of 67 Grasses (with botanical and common names) all of which have been propagated in the Botanic Gardens. I would suggest that the various local Agricultural societies would do well to procure specimens of these plants, give them a fair trial, and periodically report on them. The result would undoubtedly be the dissemination of information very valuable to the pastoral and agricultural communities.

Much interest has lately been excited by a plant called the Prickly Comfrey (Symphytum asperrimum). A number of roots of the Comfrey were purchased for the Gardens from the consignee, Mr. Cresswell, seedsman, of Swanston street. I have also received seeds of it from Dr. J. Hooker, Director of the Royal Botanic Gardens at Kew. I have raised a quantity of sets, and sent out a few specimens, including some to Dr. Schomburgk of the Adelaide Botanic Gardens. There can be no question that this plant is of very great value as a fodder plant, even if we take a moderate estimate of its productive powers. An analysis by Professor Voelcker gives the following results :—

	Leaves.		Stem.	
	In Natural State.	Calculated Dry.	In Natural State.	Calculated Dry.
Water	88·400	...	94·74	...
Flesh-forming substances	2·712	23·37	·69	13·06
Non-nitrogenised ditto	...	...	...	...
Heat and fat producing matters ...	6·898	59·49	3·81	72·49
Inorganic matters (ash)	1·990	17·14	·76	14·45
	100·000	100·00	100·00	100·00

From 80 to 120 tons to the acre is stated to be the yield of the Prickly Comfrey. Enough has certainly been adduced to render a general trial of this plant desirable. The following extract will serve to show the capabilities of this plant in a warm climate. The *Ceylon Times* of February 16, 1877, says :—

"In December last we alluded to the properties of the new fodder now coming into such general use, and which we consider so suitable for poor soils, and therefore presenting inducements for its general introduction into the maritime districts of this island. Since we then wrote we have had a long season of drought, and on all sides complaints are heard of the scarcity of fodder for cattle, though not to the same extent as in India. The following notes on the early trials with this new cattle food will perhaps give a better insight into its nature and qualities than any other account could do :—'Having procured a few sets with roots attached we planted them in a plot on the cold clay of the Forest Marble Rock, previously slightly manured These sets grew rapidly, and we were soon enabled to divide them into more than a hundred individuals as before, which were planted in like manner, and so working on till we had as much as a quarter of an acre of ground occupied, and our crop was not only abundant, but some of the stems were a considerable height, some few having been left to show its mode of growth. The rest, however, was used in various stages of growth as cattle food, though we must confess to having experienced no little disappointment on our first trials, yet no sooner did the cows (especially milch cows), horses, sheep, and pigs begin to understand it than they ate it most greedily, and our report upon it was that while all creatures seemed to thrive upon the Comfrey, yet in no instance could we find the slightest evidence of any evil effects. The crop was enormous, and this too upon land of very medium quality ; but we have this year been trying its growth on light sandy soil, and can report that all through the season of drought the deep thick roots of the Comfrey have drawn up the moisture which rises hygrometrically in our sand-bed, and the result has been a succession of green leaves when surface plants were an utter failure.'"

Another plant—the *Prosopis pubescens* (Screw or Mesquit bean of South America, the Tornillo of Sonora) attracted general attention during the past year. Through the courtesy of Dr. Hooker, I obtained a quantity of seeds of this plant; and in consequence of eulogistic notices concerning it which appeared in a portion of the Australian press, I received a very large number of applications for seeds, which were as far as possible complied with. The subjoined communications, received by the June mail from Professor Thiselton Dyer, of the Royal Gardens, Kew, show that the Mesquit bean is at least of very doubtful utility as a fodder plant, even if it be not actually hurtful; and the fact was made public—a very necessary step, since discouragement produced by fruitless labor in rearing such plants is calculated to destroy that public spirit in the cultivation of new and useful introductions which is so much to be desired.

"Sir,   Royal Gardens, Kew, May 4, 1877.

In reference to my letter, February 20, I am desired by Dr. Hooker to transmit to you the enclosed copy of a letter from the Superintendent of the Botanic Garden in Jamaica, pointing out the necessity of caution in the use of the pods of the *Prosopis pubescens* for the purpose of feeding horses.

I am, Sir, your obedient servant,

"W. R. Guilfoyle, Esq., F.L.S.,   W. T. THISELTON DYER.
Director, Botanic Gardens, Melbourne."

———

"Sir,   Cinchona Plantations, Jamaica, April 6, 1877.

I have to acknowledge the receipt of your letter dated 20th February last, informing me of the despatch of two bags containing about eight lb. of the pods of *Prosopis pubescens*, which I have also received, together with printed correspondence on the subject of these seeds.

"Some 5 per cent. of these seeds have germinated; accordingly we will have about 100 plants altogether.

"Consequent on the favourable recommendation conveyed in the aforesaid correspondence of the pods for horse and cattle food, and as only a small proportion of the seeds were in a state fit for germination, I, by way of experiment, gave about a pound of the pods to a fine healthy horse. In the morning of the third day after the pods were given to the horse the animal was found dead in the stable, and lying in such a position that left no reasonable doubt that it had died from bellyache. There are therefore strong grounds for believing that the horse thus died from the effects of these pods.

"I presume you are aware that another species of this genus, viz , *Prosopis juliflora*, a very common plant in Jamaica, the pods of which (although a valuable fodder) when eaten by horses, but especially after rains are almost invariably the means of causing severe bellyaches and very frequently death. This is attributed to the germination of the seeds in the stomach of the animal.

"Probably the above remarks may be of service by way of caution to other colonies in which this plant is proposed to be cultivated.

"I am, Sir, your obedient servant,

"W. T. Thiselton Dyer, Esq.,   "ROBERT THOMSON.
Royal Gardens, Kew."

A most estimable fodder plant is the "*Pentzia virgata*" or sheep fodder-bush of South Africa. This was also alluded to in a letter from Dr. Hooker, and is being extensively propagated in the Melbourne Botanic Gardens. From experiments I have made with the Pentzia virgata, it is no doubt well suited to the climate of this Colony, growing luxuriantly even in moist situations, though its chief recommendation is, that it flourishes in *arid* soils. It would therefore be a most valuable plant to cultivate throughout the country on an extensive scale. A letter received by me from Mr. W. Moody, of Kakanui, Otago, N.Z., states, that some seeds of *Pentzia*, which he had received, successfully germinated. He says "I have tried it here, and find it to be a good grower, and also capable of standing a considerable degree of frost. It is sometimes as low as 11 and 13 Fahr. on the ground here in winter."

A great deal has been said respecting the "Tussock grass" as suitable to this Colony. The subjoined letter, which I received from Professor W. T. Thiselton Dyer, needs no explanation :—

"MY DEAR SIR,—   "Royal Gardens, Kew, February 26, 1877.

"In answer to your letter of December 27, 1876, I enclose seeds of Symphytum asperrimum ; and at Dr. Hooker's request write to say that seeds of the Tussock grass could only be obtained for you with great difficulty, and that the trouble would hardly be justified, as Dr. Hooker is satisfied it would be of no use in your Colony. Supposing you got it established, the tussocks—which of course are only formed rather slowly—would soon be devoured and extirpated by cattle. A cow will work away at a tussock, till she has quite finished it off ; and in places where its cultivation has been attempted as a curiosity, it has had to be carefully fenced in. It is a local plant of very peculiar habits, and not at all well adapted for pasture purposes.

"Yours faithfully,
"W. T. THISELTON DYER."

Other valuable plants and seeds received were Adansonia Gregorii (the sour gourd or Cream of Tartar tree) of N. W. Australia ; Aleurites triloba (the Candle nut tree), known in the several Fijian dialects as "Lauce," "Sikeci," and "Tuitui." From the nuts of this plant a valuable oil is expressed, much employed by artists, and realising £20 per ton in Europe. Spondias dulcis (the hog plum of the Society Islands, with fruit resembling in flavor the pine apple, the leaves and bark possessing medicinal properties) ; Xanthoxylon fraxineum (the "prickly ash" or "Toothache tree" of North America, largely used in that country for rheumatic, typhoid, and scrofulous complaints) ; and very many others, a description of which would occupy too much space. Some Jute seeds, received from Charles Moore, Esq., Sydney Botanic Gardens, were sown in

September last. Seeds were germinated from one of our own plants of Encephalartos Altensteini—" the Caffer bread tree."

I have also in contemplation the formation of beds in which the principal fodder plants suitable for the Colony may be shown, and near to them specimens of the various poison plants known to Australia. Such a classification cannot fail to prove highly interesting.

The numbers of plants either quite new to the Gardens, or replacing such as were lost in former years, from June 1873 to the present date are as follows :—Genera and Species 1,213 (of this number about 120 may be considered reintroductions). Varieties and subvarieties 1,884. Total 3,097.

A Rosery is among the contemplated improvements, and will be created directly time and circumstances permit. I have secured a splendid selection of roses, and trust to make the collection of this queen of flowers a very attractive feature of the Gardens. The cultivation of such beautiful flowers as Rhododendrons, Azaleas, Camellias, &c., in public gardens is attended with a great amount of anxiety and care. We have some very choice specimens, and I hope in time to make a good display, though the buds of the Camellias planted out have at present to be rubbed off, to prevent pilferers damaging the young and delicate plants ; also to allow the shrubs time to attain a vigorous growth. A large amount of work, attended with some very practical results, has been accomplished in the Botanic Gardens' laboratory during the year. Collections of fibres were prepared and forwarded to the Queensland and Sydney Exhibitions. Among the more interesting exhibits despatched to Sydney were several novel fibres, such as *Buddlea saligna, Bromelia sylvestris* (wild pine apple); *Buonapartea juncea* (Peruvian hemp, yielding a splendid fibre) ; *Cordyline robusta* (Strong Palm Lily); *Cyperus papyrus* ("the paper reed" of the ancient Egyptians). Its valuable qualities as a *fibre* were first shown in this exhibit. It affords a fibre of firm, fine texture, closely resembling that yielded by Typha angustifolia. The qualities of the latter plant as a fibre were also first shown in the exhibits recently sent from these Gardens to the Amsterdam and Philadelphia Exhibitions. Its common name is the " native *bullrush*" or " *Cat's tail.*" It was stated in a late number of " *The Garden,*" that a company had been formed in France, with a large paid up capital, for the erection of machinery to convert the fibre of this Typha into textile fabrics. This, therefore, is another plant which might be extensively cultivated in this Colony, with important financial results. The Victorian Taper sedge, giving a very fine and strong fibre, was also sent ; Cassytha melantha (the scrub vine of Victoria, with fibre similar to that of the Musaceæ) ; *Dianellas elegans, revoluta,* and *cærulea* (the native Flax Lilies) ; *D. cærulea* (being commonly known as the Paroo Lily) ; *Doryanthes Palmeri* (Queensland Spear Lily) ; *Dasylirion glaucophyllum* (a Mexican Bromeliad, quite hardy in these gardens) ; Juncus Maritima (sea coast rush) ; sea coast Mallows ; Lavateras maritima and Olbia, yielding most beautiful fibres by a simple process of maceration, and plants to be highly recommended for cultivation as being of considerable commercial value) ; *Lepidosperma gladiatum* (sword-rush of the coast, now so favorably known and extensively used in the manufacture of paper) ; *Morœa Robinsoniana* (Wedding Flower of Lord Howe's Island) ; *Pandanus Forsteri* (Tent tree of same locality) ; Pandanus pedunculatus (Screw pine of Eastern Australia) ; *Sanseviera fasciata* (Banded Bowstring Hemp) ; *Schœnus brevifolius* (Victorian cord rush, a good fibre yielding plant, and very prolific along parts of the coast line) ; *Xerotes longifolia* (native tussock grass or Mat-rush) ; *Tritoma uvaria,* and *Tritoma recurvata* (Club-lilies)—the fibre of the latter equalling in strength and texture that of hemp. This plant is very easily cultivated, requiring no more attention than Phormium tenax. To show the rapidity with which its fibre can be prepared, leaves in full vigor on the plant at 10 a.m., were converted six hours afterwards into excellent fibre by a boiling process, at the laboratory. Some excellent castor oil has been made from seeds of *Ricinus* grown in the Gardens. Dyes were prepared from *Dais cotinifolia* (African button flower) ; *Pipturus argenteus* (Queensland grass cloth plant) ; *Sterculia diversifolia* (Victorian bottle tree) ; *Sterculia acerifolia* (Flame tree of N.S.W. and Queensland) ; *Wikstrœmia indica* (Native Daphne) ; *Baloghia lucida* (Norfolk Island Bloodwood) ; and *Araucaria Cunninghamii* (Moreton Bay hoop pine). Oleo-resin, with a most fragrant odour, was obtained from seeds of *Pittosporum undulatum.* In addition to these, and many other specimens, the largest and most diversified collection of native woods yet exhibited on behalf of Victoria was forwarded to the Sydney Exhibition ; together with a collection of Papers, also prepared in my temporary laboratory. These exhibits were accompanied by an exhaustive catalogue.

The following is a list of Exhibitions to which I have sent collections :—Melbourne and Philadelphia ; Philadelphia International ; Warrnambool ; Geelong Industrial ; Amsterdam International Horticultural ; Queensland, and Sydney.

It is satisfactory to state that in response to these efforts to make known the botanical resources of Victoria, diplomas were sent from the exhibitions, including Philadelphia.

A number of vegetable products of a similar utilitarian nature have been prepared for the approaching Exposition at Paris, and every effort will be made to have the Colony worthily represented in the Victorian Court.   The collections of woods and fibres are being largely augmented.   The results achieved with the imperfect appliances at command show the infinitely greater ends attainable if better means of operation were provided.   In last year's report a complete list was given of fibres, gums, woods, resins, &c., prepared in the laboratory and forwarded to the various Exhibitions.   An appendix to this report contains a list of Exhibits sent to this year's Exhibition at Sydney.

A wing of the New Palm house has been built, about equal in size to the present old house, which is in a very dilapidated condition.   It is to be hoped that sufficient funds will be provided to facilitate the completion of the new building, which will be an ornament to the grounds. When such is the case, the many very valuable plants now crowded together, and actually spoiling from that cause, can be placed where they can be seen to advantage.

A Calendar of the time of flowering of every plant in the Garden is regularly kept.   This will ultimately prove of great service.

The Herbarium has been considerably added to during the past year ; and amongst the many valuable additions was a fine collection of American plants, from the Smithsonian Institute at Washington.   This Herbarium has been formed during the past four years.   It now contains many thousands of species, and will soon be ready for inspection by visitors to the Botanic Gardens.   As in the case of the catalogue and label writing, a common English name will be given to each plant in the Herbarium in addition to its botanical title, and a short description with it.   I have not lost sight of the projected arboretums, to represent the trees of the five continents ; but as I am carrying out my designs from a centre and gradually extending the radius, these groups, on the extreme edge, can be postponed until work more immediately necessary is accomplished.

The number of large trees removed from the squares or obscure thickets into situations suited to their size and appearance, amounted to 820. of heights ranging from 8 to 30 feet.

The Southern District Band played in the Botanic Gardens in favorable weather, on alternate Saturdays, for the past twelve months.   The members of the band gave their services gratuitously ; and the thanks of the public are due to them for their liberality, in providing such an excellent entertainment. It gives me great gratification to state that on the last occasion, when a moonlight concert took place in the grounds, the conduct of the large number of people who attended was most orderly. So far as I could ascertain, not the slightest damage was done, even to the displacement of a label ; and the grounds might in my opinion be safely used for a similar purpose many times during the year. It is evident that an interest has been created in the public mind, concerning these Gardens, which induces visitors to aid in protecting them from the depredations of what is called the larrikin element. I have had occasion in previous reports to complain of flower and plant robberies committed in the Gardens, and in some degree these still continue, plants being taken from the borders, and even out of the houses in spite of the strict watch kept. A watchman is employed to patrol the Botanic Gardens all night, and measures are taken to ensure the watch being a vigilant one.

A rough estimate was taken of the entrance of visitors on the first Sunday of this month (June) ; the number exceeded 2,000. A very great attendance may therefore be anticipated during the more favorable seasons. I have had written and posted up in various parts of the Garden the following very excellent notice copied from one to be seen in the Fitzroy Gardens, signed by Sir Charles Gavan Duffy. The same suggestion was made by the Hon. J. J. Casey when Minister for Lands, who saw a similar notice in the Berlin Botanic Gardens :— " These Gardens were established for the recreation and enjoyment of the People ; and the improvements are placed under their guardianship." The public are thus reminded that they are the natural custodians of this national property, maintained for general recreation and instruction.

GOVERNMENT HOUSE AND DOMAIN GROUNDS.

A large amount of work has been done during the year in the private grounds attached to Government House. The borders round the base of the house, varying in width from 5 to 10 feet, had inferior soil replaced by rich earth, to a depth of 2 feet. The Fountain Court was top-dressed with good soil, and flower-beds cut out in the sward. These beds were filled with gay flowering plants, and kept up a very bright appearance during the year. The orchard was dug over several times during the year. The fruit-trees were duly pruned, &c., and are progressing satisfactorily. A cow-paddock of 10 acres was formed, which His Excellency required for his fine breed of Alderneys. To form this paddock it was necessary to remove a large number of trees, which was successfully done, the specimens being transplanted to appropriate spots. The ground was then ploughed, harrowed, and sown with English grasses. From the very inferior quality of the soil, top dressing became imperative. Several hundred loads have already been applied; but more must be done in this direction.

The large lawn in front of Government House required great attention. The necessary removal of the crest of the hill left nothing but a stiff, hard clay. About 1,500 loads of soil were carted to fill up, level, and finish the making; and 1,000 loads of manure, street sweepings, &c., were stored, to mix with 4,000 cart loads of virgin soil for a similar purpose. The contract for the latter has been let. This ground is naturally very wet and poor; good drainage is an immediate necessity; and a contract for the purpose has been commenced. The drainage of this and other parts of the ground depends so much on situation, and the nature of subsequent planting, that it requires to be left entirely in the hands of the landscape gardener. My original design, however, was to a certain extent departed from. Draining a garden is an entirely different process to other operations of the kind. Soil, situation, and purpose to which the ground is to be devoted, besides the habits of the plants to occupy the spot, require careful study. It must be remembered that drainage is one of the greatest considerations in the formation of a garden. Few people seem to be aware of the fact that proper drainage, no matter how dry the situation may be, is beneficial to vegetation, as it brings moisture to a dry spot and removes superfluous moisture from a wet one.

The large number of 4,591 young trees and shrubs were removed from the nurseries of the Garden and planted in groups around this lawn, and in the adjoining Domain.

The Croquet Lawn was completed. The borders of this, and other small lawns on the north side of Government House, were top-dressed, and planted with many choice and valuable bulbs and shrubs from various Melbourne nurseries. Near this spot a bush fern house has been built and the spot rendered very attractive.

In the Rockery and Fern Gully, numbers of Zamias, dwarf-ferns and miscellaneous plants, were used in the upper portion; all are thriving. A path was made round it, and the borders planted. The place now presents a pleasing appearance, though time will permit of further improvements. Amongst the ferns added to this gully were the following :—*Gleichenia flabillata, G. circinata, Hymenophyllum demissum, H. nitens, Trichomanes venosum, Doodia caudata, Blechnum cartilagineum, Polypodium australe, Pteris incisa, Doodia aspera,* and others.

The Footpaths, formed by the Public Works Department, on either side of the drive in the grounds, are very unsightly and are of no material advantage. Last year it was found necessary to cut off portions of them, to give effect to a requisite alteration in the drive, by which to shut out the house from the latter, at a particular spot. These paths might be dispensed with. More than 1,400 yards of walks were gravelled, and margined with gutter-tiles for surface drainage. About 400 yards of storm water drainage, were also laid, of 4-inch and 6-inch pipes respectively. Through the kindness of Mr. R. S. Inglis of Richmond a number of large specimens of *Pittosporum undulatum, P. nigrescens* and *Corynocarpus* (New Zealand Karaka), were received, and distributed through the private grounds. The whole of these grounds are much exposed to hot and cold winds ; harsh gales occasionally blow off the branches of young trees, and hence great care is necessary in selecting plants suitable to the soil and situation. Those portions of the grounds in which trees and shrubs have been planted were carefully dug over several times during the year. During the late dry summer it took nearly all the time of the staff to keep the plants alive by copious watering, and the weeds consequently made great headway, giving much afterwork to eradicate them. Water pipes are now laid all over the Government House Lawn to the various groups.

In the Domain, five iron and wooden houses were removed from near the Immigrants' Home, and carefully stacked. From these materials several out-houses for tools, &c., were built ; and the *debris* was also found very useful in patching the gardeners' houses ; a tool and cart shed 60 feet long was also built with material from the old houses. A hedge of Acacias was planted in an appropriate spot ; and 175 yards of footpaths 7 feet wide reconstructed. About an acre of ground was thoroughly trenched and drained, and added to the outer nursery in Domain ; a good substantial fence was placed around it, and there is now an excellent collection of young trees ready for planting out in spring. Near this spot 3½ acres were fenced in for a horse paddock.

The Domain greatly needs a special vote for its improvement. Before much can be done, it requires draining, trenching, levelling, and sowing with grass seeds, then the planting of pieturesque groups of trees would be attended with sueecss. So far as the means allowed, the grounds were cleaned of unsightly wattles and dead trees, and kept in order ; and an attempt was made to group some of the plants grown in the outdoor nursery. Mueh, however, eannot be done in such a large space with the present means at command.

The Prince's Bridge lake islands were cleaned and more plants added. The Yarra bank, bordering the lake, has long been the resort of abandoned eharacters of both sexes, who haunt the place day and night, making their abodes in the seedling wattles and long grass. The conduct of these people is most disgraceful and dangerous ; and the very limited staff available renders it impossible to keep them thoroughly in eheck. A few months ago one of these desperate ruffians—the common hangman—attacked a carter employed in the Gardens, and bit a piece out of his eheek. The only practical way I have found to disturb these birds of prey has been to eut away and destroy the grass and redundant vegetation in which they harbor. This has been done to a great extent, but the evil is one whieh requires thoroughly rooting out by the strong hand of the law.

The South Yarra Drive requires immediate channelling from end to end. The late heavy rains have eaused the ground to be eut up and deep ruts have been ereated. Very great damage will be caused by delay, and it is highly desirable that the Publie Works Department should take the matter in hands at once. I have asked in draft Estimates the sum of £800 for the purpose.

I have the honor to be, Sir,
Your obedient servant,

WILLIAM R. GUILFOYLE,
Curator of Botanic and Domain Gardens.

SUPPLEMENTARY DESCRIPTIVE LIST OF NATIVE WOODS PRE-
PARED AND FORWARDED TO THE SYDNEY METROPOLITAN
EXHIBITION 1877.

Botanical Name.	Vernacular Name, &c.
Acacia homalophylla (A. Cunningham)	"The fragrant Myall Wood." On the banks of the Murray river this species grows to a considerable size, the trunk sometimes attains a diameter of 18 inches, and furnishes the most beautiful wood of all the *Acacia* family. It is extensively used in the manufacture of fancy pipes, rulers, stockwhip-handles, napkin-rings, and many other articles of domestic utility or ornament. The wood is very fragrant and durable. Habitat, Victoria and New South Wales.
Banksia littoralis (Robt. Brown)	"The West Australian Coast Honeysuckle." A bushy tree attaining a height of 20 to 40 feet. Wood of a rich brown color beautifully grained ; suitable for cabinet work. Habitat, Sea Shores of Western Australia.
Cedrela Toona (Roxburgh), Syn. C. Australis (A. Cunningham)	"The Sydney Red Cedar." In the brush lands of Northern New South Wales this magnificent timber tree attains a height of 150 feet, with a stem circumference of over 30 feet, often furnishing logs 10 feet in diameter of solid wood. In India it attains to a great size; the timber is known commercially as "Chittagong wood." The bark is astringent and febrifugal and has proved a valuable agent in fever and dysentery. The flowers afford a red dye. Habitat, New South Wales, Queensland and India.
Eucalyptus corynocalyx (F. Mueller)	A tall shrub or small bushy tree ; wood hard and durable, used as fuel. Habitat, South Australia.
Eucalyptus globulus (Labillardière)	"The Blue Gum," known on the Continent of Europe as the "Fever Tree." A magnificent tree of amazing rapidity of growth. On the Bass Ranges Victoria and in Tasmania it attains to an enormous size. The timber is excellent and is much used for piles, railway-sleepers, spokes, and shafts, naval architecture and for house carpentry. The tree is now extensively planted in Italy, Algeria, Egypt, California, and many other countries not only for the value of the wood but as a preventive of fever. The deserted and fever stricken Roman Campagna has become habitable since the introduction of the "Blue Gum." Habitat, Victoria and Tasmania.
Eucalyptus sideroxylon (A. Cunningham)	The Victorian "Iron Bark"—"Black Mountain Ash" of New South Wales. A graceful tree attaining a height of 100 feet. The timber is excellent for wheelwrights' work timbering for mining shafts &c. Habitat, Victoria, New South Wales and South Australia.

SUPPLEMENTARY DESCRIPTIVE LIST OF NATIVE WOODS—
continued.

Botanical Name.	Vernacular Name, &c.
Eucalyptus fissilis (F. Mueller)...	"The Messmate." A tree of gigantic size, allied to *E. obliqua*, the "Stringy Bark ;" it is of rapid growth, and furnishes a useful though not very durable wood which is in great request for shingles, palings, quartering, battens, fence-rails and fuel. Habitat, Victoria, New South Wales and Tasmania.
Eucalyptus melliodora (A. Cunningham)	"The Yellow Box." A medium sized tree, wood of a bright yellow-color, excessively hard and tough; used for fuel. Habitat, Victoria and New South Wales.
Eucalyptus amygdalina (Labillardiére), variety regnans (F. Mueller)	The "Giant Gum"—"Stringy Gum" of the Mountains. One of the largest (if not the very largest) trees in the universe. In Gippsland trees measuring 400 feet in height are frequently met with ; exceptional specimens running up to 450 feet and having a diameter of trunk of 25 feet at the base have been found. The tree affords immense quantities of good timber ; its leaves furnish the best Eucalyptus oil. Habitat, Victoria.
Eucalyptus dealbata (A. Cunningham)	The Victorian "Grey Box"—"River Gum" of New South Wales. A medium sized tree of graceful habit chiefly met with adjacent to water ; wood hard and durable, used for fuel. Habitat, Victoria and New South Wales.
Eucalyptus polyanthemos (Schauer)	"The Bastard Box." A straggling tree of medium size, wood used for fuel. Its presence usually indicates a poor soil. Habitat, Victoria, New South Wales, Queensland and North Australia.
Eucalyptus Stuartiana (F. Mueller)	"The Victorian Apple Tree " — "Turpentine Gum" of Queensland. A graceful dense foliaged tree, height 60 to 100 feet. Wood sound tough and durable ; used for building, fence-posts, rails, fuel, &c. Habitat, Victoria, New South Wales, Queensland and Tasmania.
Eucalyptus goniocalyx (F. Mueller)	The Victorian " Spotted Gum"—" White Gum" of Gippsland A fine timber tree, found extensively on the coast, as well as inland. Wood used for building purposes, posts, rails, fuel &c. Habitat, Victoria and New South Wales.
Eucalyptus longifolia (Link) ...	The " Woolly-Butt " or " Brown Gum " of Dandenong. A handsome medium sized tree ; wood hard, sound tough and durable ; used for fencing &c. Habitat, Victoria.
Eucalyptus obliqua (L'Heritier) (variety)	The "Red Stringy Bark" of Dandenong. A fine timber tree attaining to a great height in some districts ; wood used for shingles, palings, fence-rails, building &c. Habitat, Victoria.

SUPPLEMENTARY DESCRIPTIVE LIST OF NATIVE WOODS—
continued.

Botanical Name.	Vernacular Name, &c.
Eucalyptus obliqua (L'Heritier) Syn. E. nervosa (F. Mueller)	The common "Stringy Bark." A gigantic tree often attaining a height of 300 feet, diameter of stem from 5 to 12 feet. This is one of the most useful and quick growing indigenous timber trees, its wood is very fissile and is much used for shingles, palings, fence-rails, framework of buildings and many other purposes; it is not very durable. The bark forms an excellent roofing material and is in much request amongst the settlers for this and a variety of other purposes. Habitat, Victoria South Australia and Tasmania.
Eucalyptus leucoxylon (F. Mueller)	The "Milk-White Gum" of Dandenong known also as "Spurious Iron Bark." A beautiful tree with smooth white bark; wood hard and durable, fit for railway sleepers, fence-posts, and spokes of wheels, used also as fuel. Habitat, Victoria, New South Wales and South Australia.
Eucalyptus amygdalina (Labillardière)	"The Narrow-leaved Peppermint." A tree varying much according to soil and situation, in mountainous districts it attains a great size, several forms or varieties occur one of which (*E. regnans*) has been already described. Its principal economic value is the quantity and quality of the oil afforded by the leaves. The wood is chiefly used for fuel. Habitat, Victoria, &c.
Hakea Baxterii (Robt. Brown) ...	"The Fan-leaved Hakea." A pretty shrub, somewhat resembling *H. cucullata* in habit; wood beautifully grained, hard, tough and sound. Habitat, Western Australia.
Harpullia pendula (Planchon) ...	"The Moreton Bay Tulip Wood." A fine evergreen tree; wood beautifully marked, light, sound tough, and easily worked; extensively used in cabinet making. Habitat, Queensland.

LIST OF GRASSES AVAILABLE FOR DISTRIBUTION, MELBOURNE BOTANIC GARDENS, JUNE 1877.

Botanical Name.	Vernacular Name.
Andropogon argenteum	"The Silver Beard-grass."
giganteum	"The Giant Beard-grass."
halepensis	"The Aleppo Grass."
Aira flexuosa	"The Waved Hair-grass."
Agrostis dulcis	"The Sweet Bent-grass."
Alopecurus pratensis	"The Meadow Foxtail grass."
"Alkali Grass"	
Bromus giganteus, var. longifolius? ...	"The Long-leaved Brome grass."
purgans	"The Purging Brome grass."

LIST OF GRASSES AVAILABLE FOR DISTRIBUTION—*continued.*

Botanical Name.	Vernacular Name.
Bromus ciliatus	"The Fringed Brome grass."
pubescens	"The Hairy Brome grass."
unioloides	"The Prairie grass."
marginatus	"The Margined Brome grass."
"Basuta Grass"	
Cynodon dactylon	"The Indian Doab or Couch grass."
Carex chlorantha	"The green-flowered Sedge-grass."
inversa	"The inversed Sedge-grass."
Dactylis glomerata	"The common Cocksfoot grass."
glaucescens	"The sea green Cocksfoot-grass."
Danthonia penicillata	"The Wallaby Grass."
Dichelachne crinita	"The hairy Dichelachne."
Digraphis arundinacea	"The Slate-grass."
Elymus Virginicus	"The Virginian Lyme Grass."
condensatus	"The bunch Lyme grass."
Festuca elatior	"The tall Fescue grass."
rubra	"The red creeping Fescue grass."
pratensis	"The meadow Fescue grass."
gigantea	"The Giant Fescue grass."
Scheuczerii	"Scheuczer's Fescue grass."
dimorpha	"The Jewell grass."
drimeja	"The Morning grass."
distichophylla	"The native Couch grass."
duriuscula	"The rigid Fescue-grass."
Glyceria fluitans	"The Manna or Floating grass."
Hordeum bulbosum	"The bulbous-rooted Barley-grass."
Hemarthria compressa	"The compressed Hemarthria."
uncinata	"The hooked Hemarthria."
Holcus lanatus	"The Soft or Sugar grass,"
"Kentucky Blue grass"	
Lygeum spartum	"The Broom grass."
Microlæna stipoides	"The Stipa-like Microlæna."
Milium multiflorum	"The many flowered Millet grass."
Poa ægyptica	"The Egyptian Meadow grass."
australis	"The native Wiry grass."
(variety "tenax") ...	"The tough Wiry grass."
sudetica	"The Swedish Meadow grass."
pratensis	"The common Meadow grass."
Virginica	"The Virginian grass."
Brownii	"Brown's Meadow grass."
alpina	"The Scotch Meadow grass."
Panicum plicatum	"The plaited Panic-grass."
altissimum	"The tallest Panic grass."
decompositum	"The withered Cockspur grass."
trigonum	"The three-angled Panic grass."
spectabile	"Phillips-grass," the "Caapim" of Angola.
Pennisetum longistylum ...	"The long-styled Pennisetum."
Paspalum dilatatum ...	"The spreading Paspalum."
distichum	"The Swamp Couch grass."
Piptatherum Thomasii ...	"Thomas' falling Awn grass."
Phleum pratense	"The Catstail or Timothy-grass."
Stenotaphrum glabrum ...	"The Buffalo-grass."
Stipa pennata	"The common Feather grass."
flavescens	"The yellowish Feather grass."
mollis	"The soft Feather grass."
Sporobolus elongatus	"The elongated Sporobolus."
Vilfa tenacissima	"The tough Vilfa."

APPENDIX A.

The following *Natural Orders* of Plants are now completed as far as our present means will permit :—

ORDERS ARRANGED NEAR RESERVOIR.

MYOPORINEÆ, represented by the following genera and species—
Myoporum Cunninghamii
　　deserti
　　humile
　　lætum
　　insulare
　　viscosum
　　two species not described
　　platycarpum
Eremophila bignoniæflora
　　longifolia
　　Freelingii
　　maculata
　　oppositifolia
Pholidia divaricata

ACANTHACEÆ, represented by the following genera and species—
Acanthus montanus
　　longifolius
　　spinosus
　　latifolius
Asystasia (Ruellia) ehelonoides
Barleria cristata
Belopcrone oblongata
Cyrtanthera magnifica
Goldfussia anisophylla
　　glomerata
Justicia Adhatoda
　　splendens
Libonia floribunda
　　Penrhosiensis
Meyena erecta
Peristrophe lanceolata
Ruellia Herbstii
　　longifolia
Thunbergia laurifolia
　　natalensis
Thyrsacanthus rutilans

VERBENACEÆ, represented by the following genera and species—
Cytharexylon quadrangulare
　　subserratum

Duranta elliptica
　　brachypoda
　　inermis
　　Plumieri
　　Mexicana
　　Fischeri
　　stenostachya
Lantana coccinea
　　urticæfolia
　　crocea
　　purpurea
　　mixta
　　Sellowiana
　　grandiflora
　　and a large number of garden varieties
Lippia citriodora
　　sp. Bergamot scented
Spartothamnus junceus
Verbena bonariense
　　prostrata
　　venosa
Vitex Angus-castus
　　arborea
　　littoralis
　　Lourei
Callicarpa macrophylla
　　cana
　　Americana
Clerodendron nutans
　　tomentosum

SCROPHULARINEÆ, represented by the following—
Antirrhinum majus
　　rupestre
　　assurgens
Alonson incisifolia
　　Warsczewiczii
Browallia Jamesonii
Francisca (Brunsfelsia) Americana
　　Hopeana
Buddlea dysophyllus
　　arctica
　　Madagascariensis
　　　var. canescens
　　sp. not described

Buddlea globosa
    Lindleyana
    saligna
    salvifolia
Chelone barbata
Digitalis purpurea
    canariensis
    fulva
Diplacus glutinosus
    superbus
Duboisia myoporoides
Halleria lucida
Linaria vulgaris
Maurandya Barclayana
Mimulus cardinalis
Paulownia imperialis
Penstemon Adamsonii
    campanulatum
    cordifolium
    Lobbianum
    Hartwegii
    pulchellum
    alba
    Torreyi
    cobæa
    Colvillei
    hybrida
    spectabilis
    Scouleri
    latifolius
    a great many garden hybrid va-
      rieties
Phygelius capensis
Russelia juncea
Scrophularia alpina
    frutescens
    Smithii
Verbascum Blattaria
    Thapsus
Veronica Audersonii
    Lavaudiana
    arguta
    buxifolia
    elliptica
    diosmæfolia
    formosa
    Hulkeana
    longifolia
      var. pubescens
    Derwentia
    neglecta
    versicolor
    perfoliata
    parviflora
    speciosa
    salicifolia
    spicata
    sibirica
    sarmentosa
    Hectori

Veronica cupressoides
    Schmidtii
Anarrhinum bellidifolium
Anthocercis viscosum

BIGNONIACEÆ, represented by the
    following—
Adenocalymna nitida
Bignonia Lindleyana
    Chirire
    Tweediana
    velutina
    Bungeana
    caruca
    venusta
    fulva
Catalpa bignonioides
Gelsemium sempervirens
Jacaranda mimosæfolia
Mansoa lanceolata
Oxera pulchella
Tecoma australis
      var. La Trobei
    hybrida
    grandiflora
    Mughus
    jasminoides
      var. alba
    radicans
    sorbifolia
    Stans
    ceramensis
    capensis

JASMINEÆ (including Oleineæ) re-
    presented by the following—

Jasmineæ, proper.

Jasminum didymum
    fruticans
    grandiflorum
    pubigerum
    racemosum
    revolutum
    simplicifolium
    officinale
    nudiflorum
    Reevesianum
    suavissimum
    sp. undescribed

Sub-order—*Oleineæ.*
Olea capensis
    europæa
      ferruginea
    fragrans
    ilicifolia
    paniculata

Olea verrucosa
 Wrightii
 sp. undescribed
Chionanthus ramiflorus
 virginica
Fontanesia phillyræoides
Forsythia suspensa
 viridissima
Fraxinus americana
 excelsa
  lutea
  pendula
  aurea
 floribunda
 monophylla
 Ornus
 pubescens
 sp. Canada
 quadrangulata
 sp. (Wax Ash)

Ligustrum japonicum
 glabrum
 ovalifolium
 nepalense
 undulatum
 syringæfolium
 vulgare
 leucocarpum
 sp.
Notélæa ligustrina
 longifolia
 ovata
Phillyrea angustifolia
 latifolia
 media
 oleæfolia
Syringa persica
  alba
 vulgaris
 sp.

NATURAL ORDER, GROUPED IN THE VICINITY OF FERN GULLY.

PALMÆ, represented by the following
 genera and species—
Seaforthia (Ptychosperma) elegans
 robusta
Licuala sp.
Rhapis flabelliformis
Calamus australis
Caryota urens
Ptychosperma Alexandræ
Caliptrocalyx spicatus
Latania borbonica
Jubæa spectabilis
Chamærops Fortunei
 elegans
 macrocarpa
 excelsa
 humilis
Phœnix pumilio
 reclinata
 sylvestris
 dactylifera
 spinosa
 acaulis
 leonensis
Kentia (Areca) monostachya
 Belmoriana
 sapida
Cocos plumosa
Areca sp. South America
 concinna
Pritchardia Martii
Kentia macrocarpa
 olivæformis
Sabal Adansonii
 mauritiiformis

Sabal umbraculifera
Arenga obtusifolia
Livistonia olivæformis
 sp. from Malacca
 rotundifolia
 altissima
 maritima
 (Corypha) australis
Harina caryotoides

CYCADEÆ, represented by the fol-
 lowing—
Macrozamia Miqueli
 spiralis
 Mackeni
 Perowskiana
 cylindrica
 sp. from Society Islands
 Fraserii
 Paulo-Guiliclmi
 tenuifolia
Encephalartos lanuginosus
 Lehmannii
 Altensteinii
 cycadifolia
Stangeria paradoxa
Cycas media
 Normanbyana
 sp. New Guinea
 circinalis
 Rhumphii

The Orders PALMÆ and CYCADEÆ,
 are intermixed.

ORDERS GROUPED ON NEW LAWN.

LAURINEÆ, represented by the following—

Cinnamomum zeylanicum
  Camphora
Laurus indica
  Tamala
  nobilis
  borbonia
  Cinnamomum
Litsæa dealbata
  glauca
Nesodaphne Tawa
Oreodaphne californica
Cryptocarya glaucescens
  obovata
  australis
  sp. undescribed
Tetranthera ferruginea

PITTOSPOREÆ, represented by the following—

Billardiera cymosa
Bursaria spinosa
Citriobatus multiflorus
Pittosporum cornifolium
  crassifolium
  Colensoi
  eugenoides
  revolutum
  rhombifolium
  rigidum
  phillyræoides
  tenuifolium
  Tobira
  undulatum
Hymenosporum flavum

SAXIFRAGEÆ, represented by the following—

Escallonia macrantha
  montevidensis
  organensis
  rubra
Baueria sessiliflora
  rubæoides
Itea virginica
Deutzia corymbosa
  crenata
    flore pleno
Saxifraga cæspitosa
    palmata
      Sternbergii
  hypnoides
  intacta

Deutzia gracilis
  seabra
Ceratopetalum apetalum
  gummiferum
  laurifolium
Aphanopetalum resinosum
Callicoma serratifolia
Philadelphus coronarius
  speciosus
  grandiflorus
Saxifraga rotundifolia
  sarmentosa
Tellima grandiflora
Weinmannia pauiculosa

ROSACEÆ, represented by the following—

Tribe 2.—*Drupaceæ.*

Prunus chicasa
  Cerasus
  Lauro-cerasus
  lusitanica
  Mahaleb
  Myrobalana
  serotina
  sinensis
  spinosa
  Virgiuiaua
  americana
  sp. undescribed
Cerasus ilicifolius
Amygdalus communis
  Persica

Tribe 3.—*Spiræaceæ.*

Spiræa bella
  callosa
  confusa
  carpinifolia
  salicifolia
    var. rosea
  filipendula
  hypericifolia
  opulifolia
  Reevesiana
    var. fl. pl.
  Ulmaria
  undulata
  Lindleyana
  Fortunei
  nutans var. argentea
    var rhamnifolia
  seven species undescribed
Kerria japonica
    var. fl. pl.

Tribe 4.—*Fragariaceæ*.

Fragaria vesca
Potentilla pennsylvanica
   recta
   geoides
   rupestris
   Schicatiana
   affine
   hæmatochrus
   argentea
   chrysantha
   collina
   glandulosa
Geum coccineum
   urbanum
   Wiccei
   Rafinesqueanum
Agrimonia odorata
   leucantha
   repens
   pilosa
   Eupatoria
Rubus biflorus
   Borreri
   Balforianus
   cordifolius
   eorylifolius
   dumetorum
   diversifolius
   Idæus
   laciniatus
   Lindleyaaus
   macropodus
   paludosus
   rosæfolius
   cchinatus
   rhamnifolius
   subcrectus
   thyrsoides
   rugosus
   australis
   canadensis
   sp. undescribed

Tribe 5.— *Sanguisonbeæ*.

Poterium sanguisorba
   var. minor
Acæna sanguisorbæ
Sanguisorba tenuifolia

Tribe 6.—*Roseæ*

Rosa Banksiæ
   canina
   caroliniana
   damascena
   lævigata
   nana
   rubiginosa

Rosa blanda
   spinosissima
   setigera
   cinnamomea
   var. glandulifera
   3 sp. undescribed

Tribe 7.—*Pomaceæ*.

Pyrus Malus
   arbutifolia
   aucuparia
   var. quercifolia
   Aria
   baceata
   var. aurantiaca
   var. microcarpa
   ecrasifera
   coronaria
   latifolia
   pinnatifida
   prunifolia
   var. conocarpa
   var. longicarpa
   salicifolia
   spectabilis
   5 sp. undescribed
Cydonia vulgaris
   japonica
Eriobotrya japonica
Mespilus germanica
Quillaja saponaria
Raphiolepis indica
   variety
   ovata
Photinia serrulata
Cotoneaster rotundifolia
   Roylei
   Simmondsii
   tomentosa
   vacciniifolia
   buxifolia
   vulgaris
   affiuis
   baccillaris
   microphylla
   obtusa
   nepalense
   2 sp. undescribed
Cratægus coccinea
   pyracantha
   oxyacantha
   var. laciniata
   flore rosea
   var. eriocarpa
   var. stricta
   var. obtusa
   Azarolus
   sanguinea
   punctata

Cratægus crus-galli
    var. ovalifolia
    var. prunifolia
  pyrifolia
    var. spinosa
  tanacetifolia variety
  Celsiana
    var. odoratissima
  virginica
  several undescribed species

URTICEÆ (including Moraceæ, Ulmaceæ, Cannabinaceæ, and Platanaceæ), represented by the following—

Sub-order—*Moraceæ.*

Broussonetia papyrifera
Ficus aspera
  rubiginosa
  Carica
  elastica
  lucida
  macrophylla
  macrocarpa
  nitida
  religiosa
  stipulata
  vesca
  Sycomorus
  syringæfolia
  Hardlandii
  nesophila
  lurida
  latifolia
Maclura aurantiaca
Morus alba
    var. Morettiana
    var. multicaulis
  Cape Good Hope
  nigra
  rubra
  mauritiana

Sub-order—*Ulmaceæ.*

Planera japonica
Celtis occidentalis
    var. cordata
  australis
  sp. Cape Good Hope
  rhamnifolia
Trema orientalis
Ulmus campestris
    var. viminalis
    var. variegata
    var. pendula
    var. purpurea

Ulmus moutana
    var. fastigiata
  suberosa
  chinensis
  americana
    var. pendula

Sub-order—*Cannabinaceæ.*

Cannabis sativa
    var. gigantea
Humulus lupulus

Sub-order—*Platanaceæ.*

Platanus occidentalis
  orientalis

Urticeæ proper.

Urtica ferox
Bœhmeria argentea
  macrophylla
  sp. Java
  nivea
Pipturus propinquus
Laportea gigas
  photiniphylla
Parietaria officinalis

SOLANEÆ, represented by the following—

Atropa Belladonna
Brugmansia suaveolens
    var. lutea
  Knightii
Cestrum aurantiacum
  odoratissimum
  diurnum
  nocturnum
  fœtidissimum
Chænesthes lanceolata
Datura sanguinea
  meteloides
Fabiana imbricata
Habrothamnus Ronyalli
  elegans
  scaber
  fasciculatus
  sp. undescribed
Hyoscyamus niger
Jochroma tubulosa
Withania somnifera
Lycium australe
  rigidum
  barbarum
  sp. Caffir Thorn
Nicotiana Tabaccum
  glauca
  rustica

Neirembergia frutescens
Petunia variabilis
Physalis peruviana
Solandra lævis
Solanum auriculatum
    atropurpureum
    repandum
    caffrum
    coriaceum
    Dulcamara
    glaucophyllum
    hystrix
    hæmatocarpum
    jasminoides
    simile
    laciniatum
    marginatum
    nigrum
    pseudo-capsicum
    ciliatum
    pyracanthum
    sodomæum
    robustum
    four undescribed species

PROTEACEÆ, represented by the
    following—

Banksia marginata
    Cunninghamii
    integrifolia
    ericifolia
    Hookerii
    littoralis
    Baxteri
    serrata
    Brownii
    three sp. undescribed
Grevillea alpina
    var. Dallachiana
    aquifolium
    Banksii
    confertifolia
    linearis
    oleoides, var. dimorpha
    ericifolia
    ilicifolia, var. lobata
    longifolia
    macrostylis
    obtusifolia
    parviflora
    riparia
    robusta
    Hilliana
Hakea acicularis
    Baxterii
    ulicina
    corymbosa
    crassifolia
    cucullata

Hakea cycloptera
    elliptica
    criantha
    laurina
    flexilis
    gibbosa
    leucoptera
    microcarpa
    nitida
    nodosa
    oleæfolia
    propinqua
    purpurea
    pugioniformis
    rostrata
    saligna
    suaveolens
    undulata
    verrucosa
    trineura
    orthorrhyncha
    five sp. undescribed
Macadamia ternifolia
Knightia excelsa
Leucadendron argenteum
    glabrum
    uliginosum
    sp. undescribed
Lomatia silaifolia
    longifolia
Telopia speciosissima
Stenocarpus saliguus
    variety
    sinuatus
Protea mellifera
    cynaroides
    aurea
    sp. undescribed
Dryandra plumosa
    floribunda
    sp. undescribed

THYMELEÆ, represented by the fol-
    lowing—

Daphne Houtteana
    laureola
    Mezereum
    hybrida
    indica
        alba
        rubra
Dais cotinifolia
Pimelea curviflora
    drupacea
    linifolia
    clavata
    octophylla
    humilis
    decussata

CUPULIFERÆ, represented by the
following—
Quercus robur
    var. fastigiata
  lancifolia
  reticulata
  lusitanica
    var. Mirbeckii
  suber
  spicata
  rubra
  lanata
  Hodgkinsonii
  cerris
    varieties of
  castanea
  sinuata
  Ilex
    varieties of
  coccifera
  alba
  macrocarpa
  bicolor
  Ægilops
  glauca
    variety
  lobata
  agrifolia
  serrata
  glabra
  Tauzin
  mexicana
  paniculata
  virens
  coccinea
  cinerea
  polymorpha
  carnea
  sonomensis
  tinctoria
  cuneata
  Gerhardiana
  Dalechampei
  alnoides
Corylus Avellana
Myrica cerifera

BERBERIDACEÆ, represented by
the following—
Berberis aristata
  asiatica
  buxifolia
  aquifolia
  canadensis
  stenophylla
  crassifolia
  cratægina
  Darwinii
  diversifolia

Berberis Fortunei
  fuchsioides
  Hookeri
  orientalis
  hypoleuca
  iberica
  Jamiesonii
  japonica
  laxiflora
  Leschenaulti
  macrophylla
  mexicana
  Newberti
  sp. undescribed
  pinnata
  pallida
  provincialis
  sinensis
  sanguinolenta
  tenuifolia
  trifoliata
  vulgaris
    var. lutea
    var. purpurea
Nandina domestica

POLYGALEÆ, represented by the following—
Polygala speciosa
  myrtifolia
  Dalmasiana
  grandiflora
  oppositifolia
  grandis
Muraltia Heisteria

ANONACEÆ, represented by the fol-
lowing—
Asimina triloba
Eupomatia laurina

MAGNOLIACEÆ, represented by the
following—
Liriodendron tulipiferum
Illicium grandiflorum
  floridanum
Magnolia tomentosa
  superba
  acuminata
  tripetala
  fuscata
    var. anonæfolia
  spectabilis
  grandiflora
    var. lanceolata
  Norbertiana
  glauca
  Yulan
  obovata
  Lenne

Michelia neilgherriea
    Champaca
Drimys axillaris
    aromatica
TERNSTRŒMIACEÆ, represented
    by the following —
Thea Bohea—" Black Tea"
    Assamica—" Assam Tea"
Camellia Japonica (Japanese Camellia)
    reticulata
    sasanqua rosea
RANUNCULACEÆ, represented by
    the following—
Clematis aristata
    crispa
    flammula
        var. maritima
    microphylla
    pubescens
    patens
Thalictrum aquilegiæfolium
    macrocarpum
    minus, var. elatum
    simplex
    sp. undescribed
Anemone japonica
        alba
    virginiana
    cylindrica
Ranunculus asiatica
    Breynianus
    brutius
    oreophilus
    millefoliatus
    muricatus
    Stevenii
Helleborus lividus
    niger
Aquilegia formosa
    canadensis
Pæonia arietina
    officinalis
    peregrina
    mollis

ERICACEÆ, represented by the fol-
    lowing—
Clethra alnifolia
Cyrilla recemeflora
Erica arborea
    cinerea, var. atropurpurea
            var. alba
            var. major
            var. rosea
            var purpurea
    audromedæflora
    baccans
    calycina
    ciliaris

Erica concinna
    coccinea
    cerinthoides
        var. coronata
    cruenta
    margaritacea
    multiflora
    pilosa
    Giloa
    Petiveri
    pallida
    phylicoides
    tubiflora
    urceolaris
    verticillata
    variegata
    valgaris
        var. tenuis
        var. foliis aureus
    Wilmorei
    Bowieaua
    autumnalis
    hiemalis
    nigrita
    hybrida
    Cavendishii
    persoluta
        alba
    pyramidalis, var. gracilis
    Tetralix
        alba mollis
    stricta
    rubens
    vagans
        var. graudiflora
        var. alba
    linnæoides -
    ventricosa var. Brownii
           var. breviflora
           var. minor
           var. erecta
           var. graudiflora
           var. globosa
           var. Rothwelliaua
           var. rosea
           var. magnifica
           var. superba
           var. impressa
    aristata major
    Burnetti
    coloraus
    alba, var. minor
    vernix cocciuea
    mammosa
    rigida, var. alba
    Hammoudii
    pygmæa
    Mackeyana
    Allportei
    sp. (2)

Kalmia latifolia
Menziesia polifolia
   var. alba
Rhododendron arboreum
  ponticum
  neillgaricum
  fragrantissimum
  aucubæfolium
Arctostaphylos tomentosa
  arbutoides
Arbutus Unedo
  Menziesii
  procera
  sp. (2) undescribed
Audromeda Catesbæi
  formosa
  phillyræfolia

Azalea indica
  phœnicea
  obtusa
  microphylla

EPACRIDEÆ, represented by the following—
Sprengelia cœrulea
Epacris exserta
  longiflora
  impressa
    var. carminea
    var. paludosa
    var. acuminata
Acrotriche serrulata
Leucopogon Richei
Astroloma humifusa

LIST OF PLANTS INTRODUCED INTO GARDENS SINCE JULY 1876, EITHER QUITE NEW TO THE ESTABLISHMENT OR TO REPLACE THOSE WHICH HAD BEEN LOST IN FORMER YEARS.

Those marked with an asterisk are re-introductions.

Agave Shawi
  cœrulescens
Ailanthus excelsa
Asperula azurea
Anemone cylindrica
Acer japonicum, var. rufinervum
  polymorphum dissectum, fol. roscus
  versicolor
  palmatifidum, fol. variegatum
Asclepias incarnata
Abutilon Darwiui, var. tesselatum
  Van Houttei, var. aurea
  vexillarium (megapotamicum), var. variegatum
  Auguste Paswald
Azalea La Victorie
  Chas. Encke
  Charmer
  Sigismund Rucker
  Todmanni
  Mdme. Paul Desanger
  Marquis of Lorne
  Maximilian I.
  occidentalis
Ampelopsis Veitchi
Azara microphylla
Arctostaphylos tomentosa
Abelia triflora
  arbutioides
Alstrœmeria Olympica

Aristolochia ornithocephala
  labiosa
  ciliata
  sempervirens
Adhatoda ventricosa
Aphelexis macrantha purpurea
Alternanthera Verschaffeltii
Artocarpus odoratissimus
  Lakoocha ?
Amoora Roxburghii
Alangium decapetalum
Barringtonia acutangula
Bambusa auriculata
  Tulda ?
  Balcoopa ?
Bergera Kœnigii
Begonia Mrs. Joske
  caffra
Bignonia alba-lutea
  ornata
  capreolata
Boltonia glastifolia
Bouvardia elegans
  Maidens'-blush
  Bridal-wreath
  Oriflamme
  umbellata carnea
Banksia Fortunei
  Hookeri
  paludosa

LIST OF PLANTS INTRODUCED INTO GARDENS SINCE JULY 1876,
ETC.—*continued.*

Those marked with an asterisk are re-introductions.

Berberis stenophylla
Colubrina Nepalensis
Coffea bengalensis
Carissa Carandas
*Citrus Bergamia
Coleus Mrs. Sangster
Canna Richorelli
*Candollea cuneiformis
*Cytisus Laburnum, var. purpurascens
Caragana microphylla
Calamagrostis longifolia
Codiæum (*Croton*) grande
 picturata
 Weismanni
 spirale
 Haukeri ?
 undulatum
 Goodenovii
 Disraeli
 Lord Cairns
 Lord Derby
Corynocarpus lœvigatus, fol. aureus variegatus
*Calostemma purpurea
Crotalaria laburnifolia
Cynoglossum australe
Cornus alba, var. sibirica
Cotoneaster acuminata
Cyrilla racemiflora
Chrysanthemum grandiflorum, var. intermedium
Clerodendron fragrans, var. flore-pleno
Cytisus proliferus, var. albus
Cupressus Lawsoniana, var. erecta viridis torulosa, var. variegata
Cercocarpus sp.
Catalpa Kæmpferii
Ceanothus Veitchii papillosus
Caladium Alphand
 Auguste Riviere
 Barillet
 Beethoven
 Chantinii fulgens
 Donizetti
 Jules Putzeys
 Leplay
 Mdme. Andrieux
 Maxime Duval
 Triomphe de l'Exposition
 Madame Alfred Maine
 Felicien David
Darwinia macrostegia
Dracæna fragrans
Dipladenia amœna
 Brearleyana

Dipladenia Boliviensis
Daphne elegantissima
*Duranta Plumieri, var. alba
Dillenia scabrella
 speciosa
*Dalbergia Sissoo
Elæocarpus longifolius
Eugenia caryophyllata
Eriodendron orientalis
*Eupatorium ageratoides
*Erodium cicutarium
Eupatorium Fraserii
Erythrina insignis
Erica cerinthoides, var. coronata
 aristata, var. major
 Burnetti
 vernex, var. coccinea
 ventricosa, var. erecta
 var. globosa
Eurya latifolia, var. variegata
Eulalia japonica
Escallonia sanguinea
Echeveria abyssinica
Franciscea Lindleyana
Fremontia californica
Ficus macrocarpa
 infectoria
 oppositifolia
Flacourtia cataphracta
Geum macrophyllum
Gloxinia A. Neate
 Jenny French
 Eustace Jarret
 Mrs. Bladen Neill
 Lady Duffy
Genetyllis fuchsioides
Gunnera scabra
Garrya MacLadeana
Gladiolus—20 new varieties
Hakea longifolia
Hibiscus Lambertii
*Helianthus mollis
Hæmanthus coccineus
*Helleborus niger
Hedera algeriensis, var. variegata
 latifolia, var. variegata
 var. marmorata elegaus
 var. marginata argentea
 Rhombea argentea
Heritiera macrophylla
Iberis gibraltica
Ipomœa mexicana, var. grandiflora
Jasminum auriculatum
Juglans fertilis
Jambosa sparteum
Kydia calycina

LIST OF PLANTS INTRODUCED INTO GARDENS SINCE JULY 1876, ETC.—*continued.*

Those marked with an asterisk are re-introductions.

Logania latifolia
Lespedeza capitata
Lepachys pinnata
Leptosiphon androsaceus
   densiflorus
Locastylis alata
Lonicera cœrulea
*Lapageria rosea
Lilium Krameri
   concolor
Lonicera confusa
Lactaria callicarpa
Livistonia Jenkensii
Monarda punctata
*Melicytus lanceolatus
Nycterinia selaginoides
Narcissus, var. totus-albus
   var. Constantinople
Nissa fruticosa
Nauclea Cadamba
Oxalis valdiviensis
Œnothera rhombipetala
Ophiopogon luteum variegatum
Olea americana
Pimelea clavata
Panicum virgatum
Phaseolus diversifolius
Pinus Loudoniana
Pluchea camphorata
Polygonum filiforme, var. variegata
Pelargonium—13 varieties (named)
Poinsettia pulcherrima, var. plenissima
Punica nana
*Pavonia coccinea
Passiflora
   Camdeni
   limbata
Protea aurea
Phormium Colensoi, var. variegata
Psidium aromaticum
Pterocarpus marsupium
*Ribes alpinum

Rhododendron aucubæfolium
   fragrantissimum
Rhamnus papillosus
Samalia malabarica
Sapindus emarginatus
   rubiginosus
Sterculia urens
Smilax ovalifolia
Sedum Maximowiczii
Spiræa Fortunei, var. alba
   salicifolia, var. Bethlemensis
Solanum ciliatum
Symphytum asperrimum
Sophora alopecuroides
Salvia Grahami purpurata
   Heeri
   Verschaffelti
Saxo-Gothæa conspicua, var. variegata
Skimmia oblata
Tropæolum peregrinum
Thermopsis fabacea
Thujopsis borealis, var. variegata
Tecoma pulchra
Terminalia Chebula
Tetranthera Roxburghii
Trophis aspera
Ulmus campestris, var. variegata
   purpurea
   viminalis
Verbena angustifolia
   prostrata
Viola (Lee's) " Victoria Reginæ "
Viburnum Standishii
   macrocephalum
Vitex nitens
Vaccinium Arctostaphylos
Wrightia mollissima
Yucca Whippleyi
   crenulata
   angustifolia
Zichya mollis

LIST OF DONORS.

Adet, Mons. (Curcier and Adet), Melbourne. Valuable seeds and plants.
Anderson, Mrs. Acland, South Yarra. Bordeaux Seps. (Edible Fungus.)
Anderson, Colonel, South Yarra. Large Palms.
Archer, W. H., Hawthorn. Seeds and cuttings.
Ardlie, W., Warrnambool. Quantity select plants.
Barry, Sir Redmond, Philadelphia, U.S. Plants and seeds.
Berry, G. R., South Yarra. Valuable seeds.
Beveridge, P., French Island, Western Port. Seeds.

Biram, J., Bulu Buln, Gippsland. Native ferns.
Braithwaite, Capt., Missionary ship *Dayspring*.   Very select plants from South Sea Islands.
Brisbane Acclimatisation Society (L. A. Bernays, Esq.).   Seeds.
Brisbane Botanic Gardens (W. Hill, Director).   Ferns, palms, and other plants in quantities.
Bruce, J. (Bell, Bruce, and Co.), Melbourne.   Valuable seeds.
Brunning, G., Nurseryman, &c., St. Kilda.   Valuable plants, cuttings, &c., in quantities.
Byerley, F. J., Brisbane.   Choice seeds.
Calcutta Botanic Gardens (Dr. G. King, Director).   Valuable plants and seeds in quantities.
Cape Town Botanic Gardens (J. McGibbon, Esq., Director).   Seeds.
Cartwright, R. J., Government Printing Office, Melbourne.   Seeds.
Casticau, J. B., Governor H.M. Gaol, Melbourne.   Tree guards.
Chirnside, A., Werribee Park, Wyndham.   Valuable bulbs, &c., &c.
Clarke, Sir Andrew, Calcutta (per favor Marcus Clarke, Esq.).   Valuable seeds in quantities.
Clarke, Dr. E., Emerald Hill.   Valuable medicinal plants, &c.
Clarke, Marcus, Melbourne.   Choice and valuable seeds in quantities.
Cocking, Mrs., Kew.   Seeds from Japan.
Coleman, J., Sydney.   Valuable palms, &c.
Colonial Secretary, N.S.W.   Parts 1 and 2 "*Australian Orchids*," with colored illustrations.
Coutie, J., Melbourne.   Material for packing plants.
Cowan, Miss, Prahran.   Quantity seeds, &c.
Crawford, Archdeacon, Castlemaine.   Seeds.
Curl, S. M., M.D., Rangetiki, New Zealand.   Seeds in quantities.
Dall, J., New Zealand.   Valuable ferns and other plants.
Dall, J., South Yarra.   Seeds.
Daly, W. J., Melbourne.   Valuable seeds and plants from New Caledonia.
De Pury, G., Upper Yarra.   Native seeds.
Dyer, W. T. Thisteltou, M.A., Royal Gardens, Kew, London.   Valuable seeds, &c.
Eaves, S. H., Brisbane.   Queensland ferns.
Emerald Hill Town Council.   Quantity of ferns and other plants.
Farnsworth, J., Portsea.   Quantity of native tree ferns.
Fletcher, D., Sydney.   Valuable palms, &c.
French, C., South Yarra.   Plants, seeds, specimens for herbarium, &c.
Gaggin, Mrs., South Yarra.   Seeds from Fiji.
Geelong Botanic Gardens (J. Raddenberry, Curator).   Valuable and select plants, &c., &c.
Glenn, C., Entally, Tasmania.   Choice seeds in quantities.
Gordon, Mrs., Eurobin, Ovens.   Herbarium specimens.
Gordon, T. D., Emerald Hill.   Valuable plants.
Gordon, G., Water Supply Department, Melbourne.   Choice plants.
Government Gardens, Palmerston, Northern Territory (E. Price, Esq., Government Resident).   Valuable plants.

Grahamstown Botanic Gardens (E. Tidmarsh, Esq., Director). Large and valuable palms.

Guilfoyle, J, Tweed River, New South Wales. Valuable seeds and plants.

Gull, Mrs. A. E., Guildford, Western Australia. Quantity valuable palms, seeds, &c.

Halberstaedter, A., Queensland. Seeds.

Haunecke, C. F., Rangetiki, New Zealand. Quantity of palm and other seeds.

Harding, J., Mount Vernon, New Zealand. Seeds.

Harris, J., Nurseryman, &c., South Yarra. Plants.

Harrison, J., Williamstown. Choice plants.

Henty, E. (per Mr. Saugwell), St. Kilda. Valuable plants, seeds, &c.

Hemptinne, Compte de, Belgium. Large quantity valuable seeds and bulbs.

Hobart Town Botanic Gardens (F. Abbott, Esq., Director). Plants and seeds.

Hong Kong Government Gardens (C. Ford, Esq., Director). Choice seeds.

Howitt, E., St. Kilda. Valuable and select plants.

Huber and Co., Hyeres (Var), France. Large quantities seeds, tubers, &c.

Johnson, A. M., New Zealand. Seeds.

Johnson, T., Hawthorn Seeds.

Jones, C., Richmond. Quantity plants.

Judd, T., Kew. Valuable specimen and other plants.

Kendall, F. R., Melbourne. Valuable plants, &c.

Lawrence, W., South Yarra. Seeds of Valonia Oak.

Le Jeune, P., Fiji. Rare and valuable seeds, &c., in quantities.

Lewis, C., Windsor. Quantity plants.

Lincoln, A., Melbourne. Seeds.

Lucas, R., Colac. Fern specimens (dried).

Macredie, A., Piang Hill, Lower Murray. Large wood specimens.

Marrio, Eugene, Milan, Italy. Seeds.

Maxwell, G., Albany, West Australia. Seeds.

McEwin, G, Glen Ewin, South Australia. Valuable plants.

Meehan, T. and Co., Nurserymen, &c., Philadelphia. Quantity valuable seeds.

Miller, F. B, Kew. Valuable seeds, &c.

Miller, G. G., Moyston. Seeds of native plants in quantities.

Miller, Hon. H. (per Mr. Boyce), Kew. Valuable specimen plants, seeds, &c.

Miller and Sievers, Seed Merchants, San Francisco. Valuable seeds in quantities.

Mitchell, R. S., Ballarat. Choice seeds.

Moore, H. Byron, Melbourne. Valuable seeds, also ferns from N. Territory.

Moran, H., South Yarra. Plants, cuttings, seeds, &c.

Mueller, Baron Von (per the Hon. Chief Secretary), Melbourne. Nos. 1, 2, 3, collections of Australian plants.

Morris, E. E. (M.A.), Head Master Church of England Grammar School. Valuable cuttings, &c.

Murray, J., St. Paul's School, Melbourne. Large specimen plants.

Must, T., J.P., Portland. Cuttings.

Nicholas, W., Mining Department, Melbourne. Dried fern specimens from New Zealand and seeds from Europe.

Nolan, Rev. E., St. Patrick's College, Melbourne. Valuable collections of seeds.

Park, T. K., Honolulu. Plants.

Peninsular and Oriental Steam Navigation Company (F. R. Kendall, Esq.). Free transmission of consignments.

Perry Bros., Nurserymen, &c., Melbourne. Plants.

Purchase, S., Paramatta, N.S.W. Valuable plants.

Rimmington, T., Prahran. Large and valuable specimen plants.

Robinson, His Excellency W. C. F., Governor of Western Anstralia. Valuable seeds in quantities.

Robinson, Lady, Sydney. Quantity valuable and select plants.

Rogers, Rear-Admiral U.S. Navy Department, California. Quantity valuable seeds.

Rowand, C. (C.E.), South Yarra. Native seeds, also wood and herbarium specimens.

Sargood, Hon. F. T., Balaclava. New Zealand ferns, &c.

Scott, J., and Sons, Nurserymen, Hawthorn. Valuable miscellaneous plants.

Scott, T. B., late Government Resident, Northern Territory. Plants, &c.

Shepherd and Co., Nurserymen, Sydney. Valuable plants.

Simson, Hon. R. (per Mr. Brown), Toorak. Valuable specimen plants, cuttings, &c.

Smith, E., Nurseryman, Walkerville, S.A. Large and valuable specimen plants.

Smith, J., and Sons, Nurserymen, Riddell's Creek. Select plants.

Stanway, W., South Yarra. Quantity plants.

Stevenson, G., Toorak. Quantity cuttings.

St. Petersburg Botanic Gardens (Chev. Dr. E. Regel, Director). Valuable seeds in quantities.

Stewart, A., Toorak. Plants.

Stuart, W., Penshurst, Victoria. Seeds.

Sturt, Dr., Northern Territory. Valuable seeds and plants.

Sullivan, D., Moyston. Seeds of native plants in quantities.

Sutton, J., Emerald Hill. Choice seeds.

Sydney Botanic Gardens (C. Moore, Esq., Director). Seeds.

Taylor and Sangster, Nurserymen, &c., Toorak. Select plants, cuttings, &c.

Trangmar, W. T., Portland. Seeds from N.W. Australia.

Trustees Technological Museum (per T. McMillan, Esq.), Melbourne. Valuable seeds from India.

University Gardens (per Mr. Elliott), Melbourne. Aquatic and other plants.

Vilmorin, Andrieux, and Co., Paris. Choice bulbs, seeds, &c., in quantities.

Wade, T., Middle Brighton. Large and valuable specimen plant.

Wallis, A. R., Kew. Select ferns, seeds, &c.

Watt, D., Nurseryman, &c., Richmond. Valuable and select plants.

Wilson, J., Prahran. Seeds from India.

Wilson, Rev. J. G., St. Arnaud. Large quantities native seeds, herbarium specimens, &c.

Wragg, G., South Yarra. Cuttings of valuable plants.

By Authority: JOHN FERRES, Government Printer, Melbourne.

www.ingramcontent.com/pod-product-compliance
Lightning Source LLC
Chambersburg PA
CBHW061236260626
47172CB00003B/878